# Blocks

by Michèle Dufresne

PIONEER VALLEY EDUCATIONAL PRESS, INC.

"I can make a castle,"
said Maria.
"Look at my castle!"

"Oh no!"

"I can make a rocket,"
said Maria.
"Look at my rocket."

"Oh no!"

9

"I can make a house,"
said Maria.
"Look at my house."

"Oh no!"

13

"I can make a tower,"
said Maria.
"Look at my tower."

"Yes, yes, yes!"

16